# ARCADE WORLD

## ZOMBIE INVADERS

WRITTEN BY **NATE BITT**
ILLUSTRATED BY **JOÃO ZOD**
AT GLASS HOUSE GRAPHICS

LITTLE SIMON
NEW YORK   LONDON   TORONTO   SYDNEY   NEW DELHI

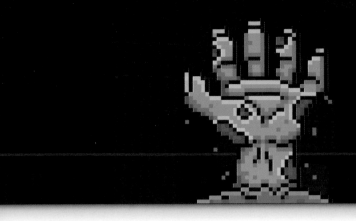

LITTLE SIMON
AN IMPRINT OF SIMON & SCHUSTER CHILDREN'S PUBLISHING DIVISION · 1230 AVENUE OF THE AMERICAS, NEW YORK, NEW YORK 10020 · FIRST LITTLE SIMON EDITION JANUARY 2022 · COPYRIGHT © 2022 BY SIMON & SCHUSTER, INC. · ALL RIGHTS RESERVED, INCLUDING THE RIGHT OF REPRODUCTION IN WHOLE OR IN PART IN ANY FORM. · LITTLE SIMON IS A REGISTERED TRADEMARK OF SIMON & SCHUSTER, INC., AND ASSOCIATED COLOPHON IS A TRADEMARK OF SIMON & SCHUSTER, INC. · FOR INFORMATION ABOUT SPECIAL DISCOUNTS FOR BULK PURCHASES, PLEASE CONTACT SIMON & SCHUSTER SPECIAL SALES AT 1-866-506-1949 OR BUSINESS@SIMONANDSCHUSTER.COM. · THE SIMON & SCHUSTER SPEAKERS BUREAU CAN BRING AUTHORS TO YOUR LIVE EVENT. FOR MORE INFORMATION OR TO BOOK AN EVENT CONTACT THE SIMON & SCHUSTER SPEAKERS BUREAU AT 1-866-248-3049 OR VISIT OUR WEBSITE AT WWW.SIMONSPEAKERS.COM. · TEXT BY MATTHEW J. GILBERT · DESIGNED BY NICK SCIACCA · ART SERVICES BY GLASS HOUSE GRAPHICS · ART BY: JOÃO ZOD, MARCELO SALAZA & WATS · COLORS BY: MARCOS PELANDRA & KAMUI · LETTERING BY: MARCOS INOUE. THE ILLUSTRATIONS FOR THIS BOOK WERE RENDERED DIGITALLY.
THE TEXT OF THIS BOOK WAS SET IN CC SAMARITAN.
MANUFACTURED IN CHINA 1121 SCP
10 9 8 7 6 5 4 3 2 1
ISBN 978-1-6659-0468-1 (HC)
ISBN 978-1-6659-0467-4 (PBK)
ISBN 978-1-6659-0469-8 (EBOOK)
CIP DATA FOR THIS BOOK IS AVAILABLE FROM THE LIBRARY OF CONGRESS.

# CONTENTS

LITTLE SIMON 2022

# CHAPTER 1

## WHERE TO BEGIN?

HOW ELSE WOULD SHE KNOW *EVERY SINGLE* TRICK IN THE BOOK?

HELLO MY NAME IS...

Totally not a secret diary, so stay out!

TIME FOR MY MORNING WORKOUT.

I SUPPOSE, TO BE THE BEST, YOU HAVE TO BE PREPARED TO FACE ANY CHALLENGE.

...CREEEEEAK

GUUUUUHHHHH...

NO MATTER HOW *SCARY.*

ALWAYS READY TO FINISH WHATEVER SHE *STARTS.*

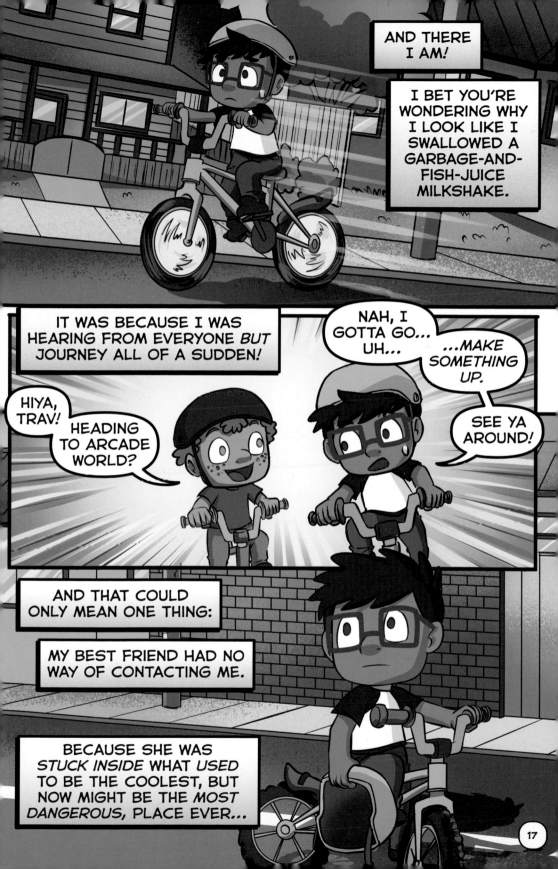

HEY, WAIT A SEC—

I THOUGHT YOU WEREN'T COMING TO ARCADE WORLD!

IS *THIS* THE FAMOUS ARCADE WORLD?! I THOUGHT IT WAS THE PETTING ZOO.

YOU'RE WEIRD, TRAVIS.

YEAH, I KNOW. THIS PLACE PUTS ME IN A MOOD.

# CHAPTER 2

NEWS FLASH: *BEAT* THEM?!

NEWS FLASH: JOURNEY, I STILL WEAR A T-SHIRT WHEN I GO SWIMMING.

SO?

PARKING LOT

SO? SO!

SO, *NEWS FLASH:* I'M NOT A RISK-TAKER-TYPE GUY.

AND ANOTHER NEWS FLASH—

UGH, WOULD YOU STOP SAYING—

NEWS FLASH!

NEWS FLAAAAASH!

PARKING LOT

NEWS FLASH: THINGS WERE ABOUT TO GET EVEN WEIRDER.

THE DEAD HAVE RISEN! AND THEY'RE INVADING THE MALL!

EXTRA! EXTRA! READ ALL ABOUT IT IN TODAY'S ZOMBIE DEADLINE NEWS!

24

# ZOMBIES INVADE NORMAL MA

Run, don't walk, to the newly redecorated Nor-Mall for a one-of-a-kind shopping experience! And remember to visit the food court so we—oh whoops, we mean, YOU—have a bite to eat! It's completely safe! Bring the whole family down.

Zombie Chef Zombino's promise: "Only serve the flesh-est ingredients!"

aaahhh!! aaahhh!! aaahhh!! aaahhh!!
aaahhh!! aaahhh!! uaaaaa.... aaahhh!!
aaahhh!! uaaaaa... uaaaaa... uaaaaa...
brainssss... aaaahhhhh... uaaaaa.....aahh
aaaahhhhh... uaaaaaa... brainssss... aahh
uaaaaa....brainsss...aaahhhh uaaaa....aah
aaahhh...uaaaaaaa...brainssss... aaahh!!!
ahhh!! aaahhh!! aaahhh!! aaahhh!!
hhh!! aaahhh!! uaaaaa.... aaahhh!!
hh!! uaaaaa... uaaaaa... uaaaaa...
sss... aaaahhhhh... uaaaaa.....aahh
hhh... uaaaaaa... brainssss... aahh
..brainsss...aaahhhh uaaaa....aah
n...uaaaaaaa...brainssss... aaahh!!!

aaahhh!! aaahhh!! aaahhh!! aaahhh!!
aaahhh!! aaahhh!! aaahhh!! aaahhh!!
aaahhh!! uaaaaa... uaaaaa.... aaahhh!!
brainsss... aaaahhhhh... uaaaaa... uaaaaa...
aaaahhhhh... uaaaaaa... brainssss... aahh
uaaaaa....brainsss...aaahhhh uaaaa....aah
aaaahhhhh...uaaaaaaa...brainssss... aaahh!!!
aaahhh!! aaahhh!! aaahhh!! aaahhh!!
aaahhh!! aaahhh!! uaaaaa... aaahhh!!
aaahhh!! uaaaaa... uaaaaa... uaaaaa...
brainsss... aaaahhhhh... uaaaaa... uaaaaa...
aaaahhhhh... uaaaaaa... brainssss... aahh
uaaaaa....brainsss...aaahhhh uaaaa....aah
aaaahhhhh...uaaaaaaa...brainssss... aaahh!!!

aa
aa.
aaa
aaal
brain
aaaah
uaaaaa

# Miss Zombie!!

aaahhh!! aaahhh!! aaahhh!! aaahhh!!
aaahhh!! aaahhh!! uaaaaa.... aaahhh!!
aaahhh!! uaaaaa... uaaaaa... uaaaaa...
brainssss... aaaahhhhh... uaaaaa......aahh
aaaahhhhh... uaaaaaa... brainssss... aahh
uaaaaa....brainsss...aaahhhh uaaaa....aah
aaaahhhh...uaaaaaaa...braiiisss... aaahhh!!!
aaahhh!! aaahhh!! aaahhh!! aaahhh!!
aaahhh!! aaahhh!! uaaaaa.... aaahhh!!
aaahhh!! uaaaaa... uaaaaa... uaaaaa...
brainssss... aaaahhhhh... uaaaaa......aahh
aaaahhhhh... uaaaaaa... brainssss... aahh
aaaaa....brainsss...aaahhhh uaaaa....aah
aahhhh...uaaaaaaa...brainssss... aaahh!!!

hhh!! aaahhh!! aaahhh!! aaahhh!!
hh!! aaahhh!! uaaaaa.... aaahhh!!
h!! uaaaaa... uaaaaa... uaaaaa...
sss... aaaahhhhh... uaaaaa......aahh
hhh... uaaaaaa... brainssss... aahh
..brainsss...aaahhhh uaaaa....aah
h...uaaaaaaa...brainssss... aaahh!!!
aaahhh!! aaahhh!! aaahhh!!
aaahhh!! uaaaaa.... aaahhh!!
uaaaaa... uaaaaa... uaaaaa...
aaaahhhhh... uaaaaa......aahh
uaaaaaa... brainssss... aahh
nsss...aaahhhh uaaaa....aah

aaahhh!! aaahhh!! aaahhh!! aaahhh!!
aaahhh!! aaahhh!! uaaaaa.... aaahhh!!
aaahhh!! uaaaaa... uaaaaa... uaaaaa...
brainssss... aaaahhhhh... uaaaaa......aahh
aaaahhhhh... uaaaaaa... brainssss... aahh
uaaaaa....brainsss...aaahhhh uaaaa....aah
aaaahhhh...uaaaaaaa...brainssss... aaahhh!!!
aaahhh!! aaahhh!! aaahhh!! aaahhh!!
aaahhh!! aaahhh!! uaaaaa.... aaahhh!!
aaahhh!! uaaaaa... uaaaaa... uaaaaa...
brainssss... aaaahhhhh... uaaaaa......aahh
aaaahhhhh... uaaaaaa... brainssss... aahh
uaaaaa....brainsss...aaahhhh uaaaa....aah
aaaahhhh...uaaaaaaa...brainssss... aaahh!!!

aaahhh!! aaahhh!! aaahhh!! aaahhh!!
aaahhh!! aaahhh!! uaaaaa.... aaahhh!!
aaahhh!! uaaaaa... uaaaaa... uaaaaa...
brainssss... aaaahhhhh... uaaaaa......aahh
aaaahhhhh... uaaaaaa... brainssss... aahh
uaaaaa....brainsss...aaahhhh uaaaa....aah
aaaahhhh...uaaaaaaa...brainssss... aaahh!!!
aaahhh!! aaahhh!! aaahhh!! aaahhh!!
aaahhh!! aaahhh!! uaaaaa.... aaahhh!!
aaahhh!! uaaaaa... uaaaaa... uaaaaa...
brainssss... aaaahhhhh... uaaaaa......aahh
aaaahhhhh... uaaaaaa... brainssss... aahh
uaaaaa....brainsss...aaahhhh uaaaa....aah
aaaahhhh...uaaaaaaa...brainssss... aaahh!!!

## The Best Zombie Barbershop!

AND WITH THAT LITTLE PEP TALK OUT OF THE WAY, WE WERE OFF TO FACE THE ZOMBIE HORDE.

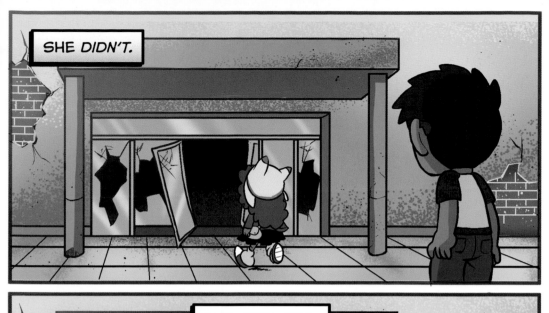

SHE *DIDN'T.*

BUT SHE WENT IN ANYWAY.

AND SO DID I.

THE ZOMBIES HAD INVADED, ALL RIGHT...

...AND THEY WERE HERE TO SHOP TILL THEY DROPPED.

PYOOOOOM!

SMASH!

-SM

-SMAAASH!

-SM

-SMASH!

VRRRRR!

IS THAT A DRONE?

46

WHOA! GUESS WE'RE LEVELING UP.

AND I DIDN'T EVEN GET A MALL PRETZEL.

WHO NEEDS A MALL PRETZEL WHEN YOU CAN HAVE *THAT?!*

IT CAN'T BE! WE GOT THE—

HIGH SCORE! MUD SHOVEL... UNLOCKED!

MUD SHOVEL!

I CAN FEEL ITS AWESOME POWER.

I CAN SENSE ITS MAGIC...

I...HAVE NO IDEA HOW TO USE IT.

CHAPTER 4

BEATING THE EARTH ZOMBIES MADE US FEEL LIKE WE WERE ON TOP OF THE WORLD.

THEN MONDAY HIT. AND THAT FEELING WAS...WELL, *HISTORY.*

BELIEVE IT OR NOT: I MISSED THE EXCITEMENT OF BATTLING ZOMBIES.

SO MUCH SO, I STARTED SEEING THEM EVERYWHERE.

BENJAMIN FRANKLIN BECAME ZOM-BENJAMIN FRANKLIN.

AND HISTORY CLASS BECAME A DISTANT MEMORY RIGHT BEFORE THE BELL.

RIIIIIING!

I'LL BITE: WHAT'S THE SCOOP?

WIND ZOMBIES HAVE INVADED THE FLY ZONE!

UGH. WIND ZOMBIES ARE THE WORST!

TELL ME ABOUT IT!

MY COUSIN IS A WIND ZOMBIE.

I SAY TODAY IS MONDAY, AND THE FLY ZONE IS CLOSED ON MONDAYS. WHICH YOU WOULD KNOW...

...IF YOU FOLLOWED THEM ONLINE.

*MEGABYTES!* I WAS READY TO TAKE ON ANOTHER VID-WORLD.

AFTER DUSTING THOSE LEVEL-ONE CREEPS, THIS WOULD HAVE BEEN A *BREEZE*...

# CHAPTER 5

THERE YOU ARE! YOU MISSED IT.

WE GOT THE *WIND RING!*

YOU CAN KEEP THE WIND RING.

I JUST WANT MY NOTEBOOK BACK.

WHAT IS SO SPECIAL *ABOUT* THESE?

THE TOWN OF NORMAL EXPERIENCED WHAT GROWN-UPS CALLED "AN ELECTRICAL DISTURBANCE" THAT NIGHT.

OH GREAT, NOW I'M GONNA HAVE NIGHTMARES.

THIS WASN'T JUST WI-FI GOING OUT.

PEOPLE WERE SEEING STRANGE STUFF ALL OVER.

EVERYONE LOST POWER FOR EXACTLY TWELVE MINUTES.

BUT ONE PLACE, SOMEHOW, *MAGICALLY* STAYED ONLINE WITHOUT A BLIP.

# CHAPTER 6

WHO TURNED OUT THE LIGHTS?

YEAH, SERIOUSLY, DID THE ZOMBIES TAKE OUT THE POWER GRID?

YOU KIDS SHOULD REALLY GET HOME.

POWER'S OUT. IT'S NOT SAFE.

WE WILL, MRS. MARTINEZ!

WHY IS THE SPRINKLER ON?

FT·T·T·T·T·T!

FT·T·T·T·T·T·T·T·T!

AAAAAAHHHH!

ZOMBIES WEREN'T AWFUL ENOUGH?

NOW, THEY'RE JELLYFISH, TOO?

THIS IS DEFINITELY *NOT* FROM THE GAME.

I'M GUESSING *THEY'RE* NOT EITHER!

HOP!

THUD

QUICK, SLIDE!

HOP!

JACKPOT! WE'RE SAVED.

NOW, POGO LIKE YOUR LIFE DEPENDS ON IT.

HAVEN'T WE HAD ENOUGH BOUNCING FOR ONE DAY?

# CHAPTER 7

AFTER THE LONGEST MINUTE OF OUR LIVES, WE FINALLY SAW THE LIGHT...

THE POWER RETURNED TO NORMAL.

OH, THANK HEAVENS, THE WI-FI IS BACK ON!

WOO-HOO! WE'RE GONNA BE OKAY, KIDS!

BLUB!

BLUB!

BLUB!

BLUBBB!

I DON'T THINK WE WON.

IN THE GAME, YOU HAVE TO FLUSH THE WATER ZOMBIES DOWN THAT GIANT TOILET, REMEMBER?

WHICH DOESN'T MAKE A WHOLE LOTTA SENSE.

WOULDN'T THAT MAKE THE WATER ZOMBIES *MORE* POWERFUL?

DUNKING THEM IN MORE WATER?

UH-OH—

HANG ON!

RUMMMMMMBLE

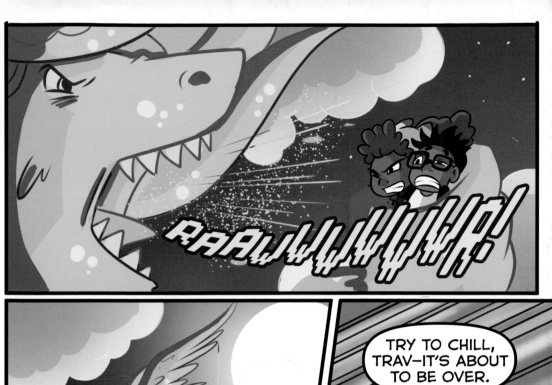

115

AND THAT'S HOW WE GOT TRAPPED IN A FIRE MAZE...

SPLIIIIIIISH!

WE GAVE THE FIRE ZOMBIES EVERYTHING WE HAD.

WE TRIED *WATER*...

HISSSSS!

...BUT THAT ONLY MADE THEM A LITTLE *STEAMED*.

AND I MEAN *LITTLE*.

THE MUD SHOVEL SHOULD HAVE WORKED...

...BUT THIS VID-WORLD WAS PLAYING *DIRTY.*

THE FIRE ZOMBIES FOUND THEIR WAY TO US AGAIN*!*

I HOPE THIS WORKS!

*WIND RING!*

WOOOOOSH!

126

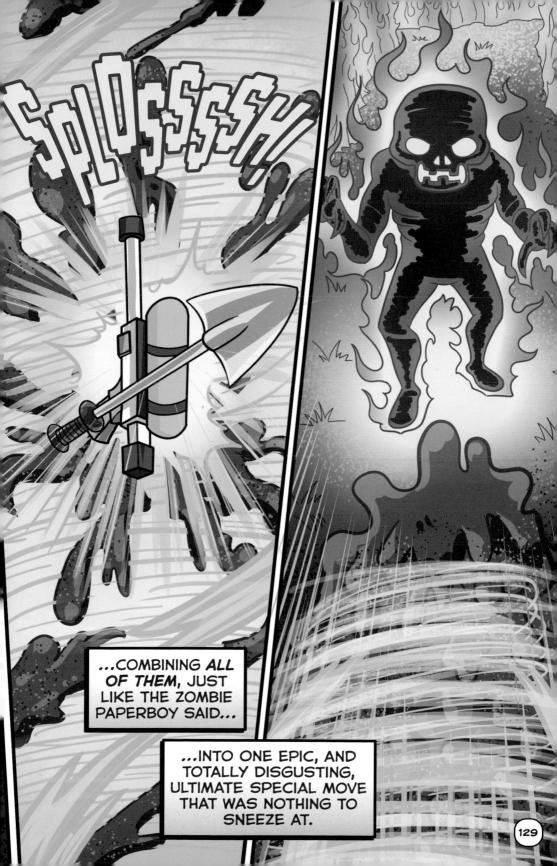

SPLOSSSSH!

...COMBINING *ALL OF THEM*, JUST LIKE THE ZOMBIE PAPERBOY SAID...

...INTO ONE EPIC, AND TOTALLY DISGUSTING, ULTIMATE SPECIAL MOVE THAT WAS NOTHING TO SNEEZE AT.

WELL, IF THERE'S SUCH A THING AS A HIGH SCORE IN *ZOMBIE INVADERS*, WE JUST SHATTERED IT.

COULDN'T HAVE DONE IT WITHOUT YOU...

...AND YOUR ALLERGIES.

PLAYER ONE...

PLAYER TWO...

BLOW IT UP!

# CHAPTER 10

135

136

# CAN'T GET ENOUGH OF ARCADE WORLD? CHECK OUT THE NEXT ADVENTURE...

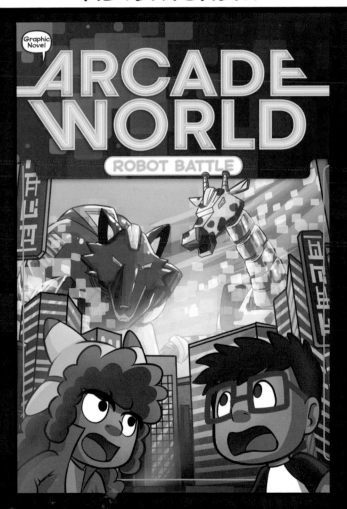